HERE THEY COME!

DAVID COSTELLO

Farrar Straus Giroux

New York

Distributed in Canada by Douglas & McIntyre Ltd.
Color separations by Chroma Graphics PTE Ltd.
Printed and bound in the United States of America by Phoenix Color Corporation
Designed by Nancy Goldenberg
First edition, 2004
1 3 5 7 9 10 8 6 4 2

www.fsgkidsbooks.com

Library of Congress Cataloging-in-Publication Data
Costello, David.
    Here they come! / David Costello.— 1st ed.
        p.   cm.
    Summary: When a group of frightening creatures holds a Halloween party in the woods,
some costumed children give them a scare.
    ISBN 0-374-33051-4
    [1. Halloween—Fiction.   2. Stories in rhyme.]   I. Title.

PZ8.3.C82827He 2004
[E]—dc21

                                                                        2003045510

Here comes our chance for a Halloween fright,
For this is the place every Halloween night
Where the scariest creatures are known to appear,
And that's why the party is here every year:
Where the path in the woods takes a bend and a turn,
Round a circle of stones where a fire can burn
And light up the scene by the old hollow tree.
It's an excellent place for a party to be.

Mom says, "You children are in for a treat.
A good scare can knock you right flat off your feet
And make your eyes pop and your heart beat like thunder."
She says that it's fun, but we do have to wonder.

She says that a scare lets you know you're alive.
Now listen! The guests are about to arrive!

Here come some warlocks, here come the ghosts,
Here come the witches, greeting the hosts.

Then it's a scarecrow with corn for the cookout,
Along with an owl who will keep a keen lookout.

Here come some hopping hobgoblins hobnobbing,
With pumpkins for carving and apples for bobbing.

Werewolves arrive with two ghouls and a bat,

Then good old Hornaby—he's mostly hat.

A walking bush enters and meets with a sprite.

Then in comes the thing that goes bump in the night.

Gremlins come waddling, followed by trolls.

An ogre comes strolling with cinnamon rolls.

A couple of phantoms appear from thin air.

They must come from someplace, but we don't know where.

What's that? A marsh monster straight from the source.

What's in his basket? Marshmallows, of course.

Here come musicians, playing and singing . . .

Now this party is really swinging!

Everyone's jumping to join in the dance.
Hatless, old Hornaby's nothing but pants.

Get your corn roasted, or just eat it raw,
But you have to watch out when you're made out of straw.

A hobgoblin bobbing for apples has bitten
A dragon who's hiding from some witch's kitten.

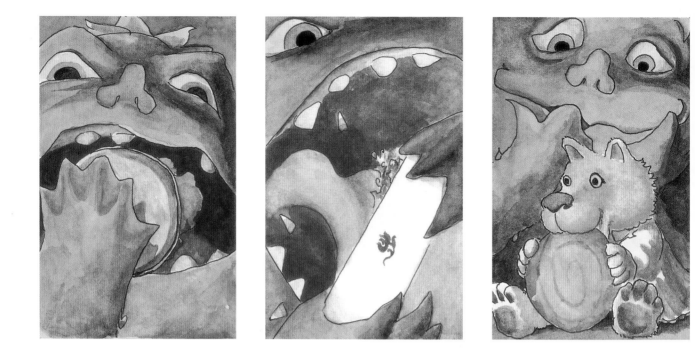

The marsh monster swallows a pumpkin pie whole,
Then chomps down the candy corn, bowl after bowl,
Then licks up a dish of squished fish casserole,
But the little wolf gets the last cinnamon roll.

Next, overhead, a bright sparkle and glow—
The witches have started to put on their show.

Now the great ghost storyteller delivers

A tale to give anyone listening the shivers

Until we're scared silly, and then comes the call:

That *was* a fun scare—

our mother was right.

See you next year on Halloween night!